Scarlet SILVER

Freda the Fearless

Original concept by Sarah McConnell
Written by Lucy Courtenay
Illustrations by Sarah McConnell

Hodder
Children's
Books

A division of Hachette Children's Books

Contents

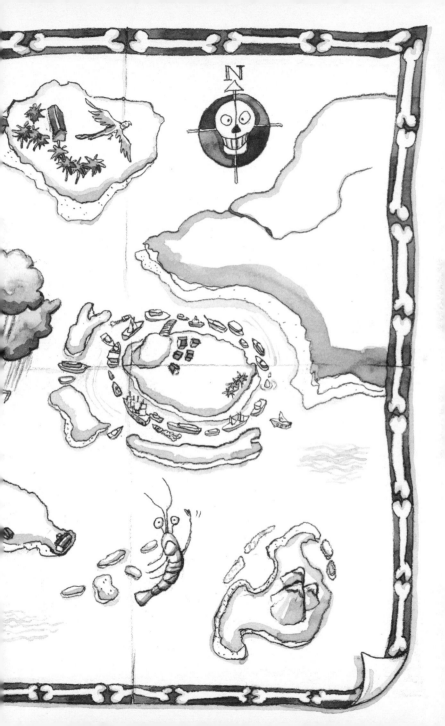

A Knock on the Head

Somewhere in the middle of the Seven Seas, a small blonde pirate lay on her hammock with her hands behind her head, staring at the ceiling. Or rather, staring at the treasure map that was stuck to the ceiling.

The map was half finished. On one side, there were drawings of islands, storms, waves, ships, fish and – oddly – space rockets. On the other half, there was nothing. Just a cut-out shape of a pirate ship stuck down with Blu-Tack and a big fat question mark.

"We're sailing into the unknown, Bluebeard," Scarlet Silver sighed. "If only Granny had been clearer about this tremendous treasure hunt, instead of leaving us a riddle to solve! We've still got two more parts of the riddle to work out, and I don't know how we're going to do it."

"Fart," said the small blue and yellow budgie perched on the tip of Scarlet's purple pirate boot.

Scarlet frowned. "Has Lipstick been teaching you rude words again, Bluebeard?"

A large parrot flew into Scarlet's cabin in a flurry of red feathers.

"Bottoms!" Lipstick screeched, before turning and flying out again.

"Fart!" said Bluebeard happily. He flapped up to the lantern that swung from the cabin roof.

Scarlet rolled on to her tummy. This is difficult to do when you are in a hammock, but Scarlet had had plenty of practice. She took off the large green pendant that was hanging around her neck. Then she took two small blue puzzle pieces out of her pocket, and laid them in two corners of the pendant like a jigsaw. The magnets clicked into place.

"Two more parts of the riddle to solve," Scarlet said to herself. "Two more pieces of this puzzle to find. Then maybe we'll know what this tremendous treasure hunt is all about. And I can add a few more details to my map."

Scarlet had always drawn treasure maps. But this was her first *real* treasure map, because she'd only just discovered that her family were *real* pirates. Now Scarlet was captain of her grandmother Long Joan Silver's old pirate ship *55 Ocean Drive*, and her family (plus Grandpa Jack's best friend One-Eyed Scott, Ralph the ship's cat, Bluebeard and Long Joan's old parrot Lipstick) was the crew. It worked very well – at least, most of the time.

Scarlet took down her map and

frowned at it. Something wasn't right.

"CEDRIC!" Scarlet yelled. "Did you draw space rockets on my map?"

A small boy pirate in glasses and an alien-print bandana stuck his head through Scarlet's cabin door.

"Yup," Cedric said. "Do you like them, Scarlet?"

"Scribbling on the captain's map is against the pirate code," Scarlet said crossly. "I know you're space crazy, but what if future pirates use my map and think they are going to find aliens?"

"I wish," Cedric said.

"I should lock you in the brig," Scarlet continued. The brig was a large cage onboard ship, used for putting naughty pirates in.

"You could try," said Cedric cheerfully.

"But I've just developed a new lock-picking gadget that would get me out before you could dance half a hornpipe. Which reminds me. Mum says to come up on deck. It's time for hornpipe practice."

The hornpipe was a cross between a dance and a keep-fit session for pirates. Scarlet knew that keeping fit while at sea was very important. But she couldn't help wishing they could do without hornpipe practice, just for today. She had too much on her mind.

She followed her brother out on deck.

"Mum," Scarlet said to the red-haired lady pirate tuning her accordion in the shade of the mainmast. "The next part of Granny's riddle—"

"I've had a bright idea about that, Scarlet," said Lila Silver, sounding pleased. She pressed a few buttons on her accordion, which went *skwinkle-winkle*. "You'll see in a minute."

"It's not like that bright idea you had about ironing the ship's sails while they were still on the masts, is it Mum?" Scarlet asked cautiously.

"This idea is *much* better," said Lila.

Scarlet sighed. "OK," she said. "So, is the whole crew assembled and ready to dance? Dad?"

"Here, captain!" called Melvin Silver, tightening the laces on his pirate boots and then straightening his twisty straw-like moustache. Ralph the ship's cat was sitting firmly on top of his head.

"Grandpa Jack?"

"Aye, captain!" said an old man in a large jumper with a fish knitted on the front.

"One-Eyed Scott?" said Scarlet.

"Hornswoggling hornpipe," growled One-Eyed Scott, fiddling with some smelly-looking chicken bones in his long black hair. "Last time we done it, I put me back out."

"Perhaps you should do it less

vigorously, One-Eyed Scott," Lila
suggested.

"No point in hornpiping 'less you
throws yourself into it," One-Eyed Scott
said with a sniff.

"Ready, Cedric?" Scarlet asked.

Cedric stood up from tweaking
something on the leg splints that he wore
to help him walk. "I'm testing out my
new hornpipe attachments today," he
said. Cedric was always inventing new
gadgets. "Ready when you are!"

Lila cleared her throat. "Before we
begin," she said, "I've written a new song
for you all to dance to. It's called *Up on
High*. I got my inspiration from the third
part of Lipstick's riddle about the
tremendous treasure."

"Underwater, overboard, up on high

and wave the sword!" Lipstick screeched from up on the yardarm.

"Thank you, Lipstick," said Lila. "I was also a bit hungry when I wrote it, as you will see. I hope that the words will make you think about high-up places where the third puzzle piece might be hidden."

"Great, Mum," said Scarlet, feeling impressed. "Take it away!"

Lila pressed a few more accordion buttons. The accordion went *squnkle squink*. "*Up on high, up on high*," sang Lila. "*Sunshine smoothies, seagull pie, tap your toes and work out why Granny Joan says up on high!*"

It was a catchy tune. Soon the whole crew was dancing.

"Up on high," sang Scarlet, tapping the tips of her purple pirate boots.

"Seagull pie," boomed Grandpa Jack, doing something complicated with his arms.

"*Up on high, up on high,*" Lila sang, moving on to the second verse. "*Rainbow biscuits—*"

There was a *squoing* sound that wasn't Lila's accordion. Scarlet stared as Cedric's legs started doing something very fast and very dangerous.

"Help!" Cedric shouted. "My hornpipe attachments are stuck!"

Everyone dived out of the way as Cedric whirled down the deck in a blur of legs and alien-print bandanas.

"Get out of the way, One-Eyed Scott!" Cedric shouted.

"Rainbow biscuits," sang One-Eyed Scott. He was dancing so vigorously that

he didn't see Cedric
hurtling towards
him.

There was a
blur of arms
and legs, and then
a cloud of smoke.

C ... C ... CRUNCH

"Are you both all right?" Scarlet asked, rushing to where Cedric and One-Eyed Scott lay tangled in a heap. The rest of the crew rushed after her.

"Yeah," Cedric panted. "My feet are a bit hot, though."

Scarlet pulled One-Eyed Scott to his feet. He was looking dazed, and his eyepatch was on the wrong eye. Scarlet lifted up the eyepatch and waved her hand. "How many fingers am I holding up, One-Eyed Scott?" she said urgently.

"Fingers?" said One-Eyed Scott in a strange voice.

"One?" said Scarlet. "Two?"

One-Eyed Scott giggled. "Three, four five," he sang. "Once I caught a shrimp alive … "

"Is he OK?" Melvin asked.

"He doesn't look right," Lila said, shaking her head.

"Talk to me, One-Eyed Scott," said Scarlet anxiously.

"Who's One-Eyed Scott?" said One-Eyed Scott.

Rigg Isle

"What are we going to do?" Lila asked for the hundredth time since One-Eyed Scott's accident.

Scarlet and her crew sat around One-Eyed Scott's hammock. The old pirate was humming gently to himself as Grandpa Jack held his hand. Lipstick and Bluebeard swung side by side on the hammock ropes beside One-Eyed Scott's balding head.

"I quite like him like this," said Melvin, stroking Ralph. "He's much more cheerful than usual."

"How can you say that, Dad?" Scarlet said. "He's lost his memory!"

"Tum tee tum," One-Eyed Scott hummed.

"Should we trying slapping him round the face for a bit?" said Lila.

"Don't do that, Mum," Scarlet advised. "We need to find an island with a doctor on it."

Scarlet left One-Eyed Scott's side and went to search in her captain's locker for a chart. Returning to the cabin, she spread the chart out on the floor. The rest of the crew peered over her shoulder.

"We're a long way from the mainland," said Scarlet, tracing a line with her finger. "The rest of these islands look too small for people to live on them, don't you think?"

"What about that one?" Cedric suggested.

He pointed at an oddly-shaped island near the bottom of the map. It was larger than the other islands in the area, and seemed to have square edges.

"Rigg Isle," Scarlet read. "I've never heard of it."

"It's the biggest island in these parts," said Melvin. "I think it's our best hope."

"What if we meet Gilbert Gauntlet?" Lila asked. "We have a habit of bumping into him whenever we reach land. He'll have a bone to pick with us for scuppering his latest scam, when he robbed all those old pensioners aboard the *Matey M'Lad*."

"Bumping into Gilbert Gauntlet might be good," Cedric pointed out. "Although he's the worst villain in the Seven Seas, every time we meet him we solve another part of Granny's riddle about the treasure, don't we?"

"You're right, Cedric," said Scarlet, rolling up the chart. "Rigg Isle is worth a try. Set a course for east by south-east."

"What?" said Lila, who wasn't very good at pirate directions.

Scarlet pointed out of One-Eyed Scott's porthole. "That way, Mum," she said patiently.

55 Ocean Drive raced with the wind, which was being kind for once and blowing in exactly the right direction. Steering with one hand, Scarlet consulted the chart.

"Cedric?" she called up to the crow's nest. "Rigg Isle should be coming up soon. Can you see anything?"

"There's something all right," Cedric yelled down. "But it doesn't look like an island. Come and see for yourself, Scarlet, if you don't believe me."

Lila took the wheel, and Scarlet shimmied up the rope to the crow's nest right at the top of *55 Ocean Drive*. Squeezing in beside Cedric, she gazed at the horizon.

Something very odd was coming into view. It was black, red and brown, and stuck out of the sea at a strange angle. Peculiar-looking trees sprouted all over it. Taking out her telescope, Scarlet had a closer look.

"Rigg Isle is an *oil rig*!" she gasped. "Somehow, they got the name muddled up on this map!"

With the telescope's help, Scarlet could see that the peculiar-looking trees were the oil rig's bristling cranes and pulleys. The rig was tilting sideways towards the sea, and the whole thing was patched

with barnacles and draped with seaweed.

Scarlet jumped on to a rope and whizzed back down to the deck to tell the others.

"It don't sound like the kind of place with doctors," said Grandpa Jack.

"I still think we should give it a try," Lila said.

"Let's take a vote," Scarlet suggested. "All those in favour of landing on this old oil rig?"

Everyone stuck up their hands. Ralph
stuck up his tail.

"Farting fruitbats," Lipstick said,
clicking his beak.

"Fart," Bluebeard added, like a small
blue and yellow echo.

"Oh a-sailing we will go," One-Eyed

Scott sang dreamily, twiddling his chicken bones.

"Right," said Scarlet. "For One-Eyed Scott's sake, let's do it!"

The oil rig stood on one huge iron leg, like an extremely fat and very rusty flamingo. As they sailed closer, Scarlet could see a flight of iron steps zigzagging up the leg and out of sight. There was no harbour, and no other ship in sight. It looked like visitors weren't encouraged.

Leaving Ralph on board to guard the ship, the Silvers and One-Eyed Scott sailed their dinghy to the bottom of the iron steps and jumped ashore.

The first thing Scarlet noticed was the mice. They were everywhere. Swarming up and down the steps and chattering to each other in high voices, they were almost cute – if there hadn't been so many of them.

"We should have brought Ralph," said Melvin, looking around him.

"Too late for that," said Scarlet, as she climbed upwards.

The noise of everyone's feet on the iron

steps boomed out across the sea. *Clang.*
Boom. Clang.

"Boom," sang One-Eyed Scott woozily.
"One look at you and my heart goes
boom."

"It's hard to get into this place without
being noticed," said Cedric.

"I think that's the whole idea," Scarlet
said. "Look!"

A pirate about the same age as
Cedric stood at the top of the iron
steps. He had a very clean red and
white bandana tied around his head.
Blond ringlets fell to his shoulders,
brushing past a pair of shiny golden
earrings.

Scarlet tensed, ready to use her
kung-fu arms if necessary.

But the clean young pirate beamed at them. "Hello," he said. "Welcome to our oil rig. I'm so pleased that you've come. Did you have trouble finding us?"

Scarlet blinked.

Thoughts of kung-fu arms faded away.

"What charming manners," Lila said. "Listen and learn, Scarlet."

"Fart," said Bluebeard darkly, from his usual position on Scarlet's hat.

"You're very kind," said the pirate to Lila. "Mind the mice. They can trip you up if you're not used to them. Someone nearly fell into the sea last month."

He held out his hand and helped Scarlet and her crew up on to the oil-rig platform. The mice swarmed around their feet like a huge, moving blanket of soft brown fur.

"I can't tell you how nice it is to see you," he said happily. "I'm Horris. We don't get many visitors, and—"

"*HORRIS!*" came a very loud voice. "ARE THOSE *MANNERS* I'M HEARING? WE DON'T STAND FOR *MANNERS* HERE AT GULLIBLE GRAMMAR!"

A Big Mistake

Standing behind Horris was the largest, angriest, ugliest female pirate Scarlet had ever seen. Thick grey hair lay like a greasy mat on her head, tucked under a skull-shaped pirate hat. Her belt bristled with weapons. Half-a-dozen mice sat on her shoulders and she had a face like a boiled potato.

"Hello, Freda," squeaked Horris.

"DON'T YOU HELLO ME!" roared Freda.

"WHERE'S YOUR FEARSOME ROAR?"

"Er," said Horris, blushing rather hopelessly. "Rar?"

"That wouldn't even scare Ralph," Lila whispered to Scarlet.

"WHERE'S YOUR CURSING?" Freda yelled, drawing a shiny cutlass. "YOUR SNARLING AND YOUR YO-HO-HO-ING? CALL YOURSELF A PIRATE?"

Horris swallowed. He turned back to the Silvers. "I'm really sorry about this," he said. "But I have to call you something rude now. It's all part of my pirate education."

He cleared his throat unhappily, and raised his voice. "What's your business on our oil rig, you … poopy … parsnips?"

It was perhaps the worst pirate curse Scarlet had ever heard. Cedric sniggered.

"Shh," Scarlet whispered. "Can't you see that Horris is doing his best?"

"SCARPER, YOU STINKING LITTLE SKUNK!" Freda barked at Horris. "I'LL DEAL WITH THIS LOT."

Horris bent his head and scurried away. Freda waved her cutlass menacingly after him. Scarlet noticed that a pirate fist clutching a wad of cash was engraved on the blade. *Gilbert Gauntlet's mark.* Their pirate instincts had been right after all! Gilbert Gauntlet was involved here – somehow …

"So," the pirate growled at Scarlet and her family. "State your business or I'll slit your throats. Every last one of you!"

Freda was terrifying up close. Scarlet's tongue felt like it was glued to the roof of her mouth. She tried to make the word "doctor" come out, but only managed something that sounded like "wimble".

Freda looked over the top of Scarlet's head at Melvin and Lila.

"Hopeless pirate kids, is it?" she barked. "You've come to the right place. We get plenty of 'em here. Parents at their wits' ends. Kids that can't curse for their lives, have no interest in throat-cutting and prefer *books* to swashbuckling. Books!" She leaned in towards Cedric. "You look like a kid what likes books," she said with a sneer. "Are you?"

"Well, yes," said Cedric. "But—"

"HA!" Freda roared. The mice on her shoulders squeaked at the noise and hid in her hair. "It's education time for you two, and no mistake!"

She clapped two enormous hands on Scarlet and Cedric's shoulders and began to march them away.

"But," Lila began.

"Look here," said Melvin and Grandpa Jack at the same time.

"La la la," sang One-Eyed Scott.

Scarlet tried to explain, but her voice seemed to be stuck.

"It's always tough, seeing your precious little ones off to school," Freda bellowed as she frogmarched Scarlet and Cedric away. "But it's for the best. Fees at Gullible Grammar are payable at the end of term. Four hundred golden groats bed and board, with extra swearing lessons additional. Come and fetch 'em around Christmas time. They'll be changed beyond recognition, and maybe you'll have a pair of pirates to be proud of!"

Scarlet unstuck her voice at last. "There's been a mistake," she panted, kicking out with her purple pirate boots. Bluebeard lost his grip on her hat. "Let me and my brother go, or I'll—"

"Don't worry about a thing!" Freda called back to the Silvers, not listening to Scarlet.

"But it's all a mistake!" Lila implored.

"I've got it all in hand!" Freda repeated. "Your kids are safe with me!"

"Can't she hear what Mum's saying?" said Cedric furiously.

"I guess listening isn't her strong point," Scarlet said.

Leaning across to a metal box set into the oil-rig wall, Freda pressed a button. There was a rusty squeal of old machinery deep below Scarlet's feet. Huge spiky metal teeth rose up from the floor like a portcullis, separating Scarlet and Cedric from the rest of the family. There wasn't even time to say goodbye.

"Mum!" Cedric yelled. "Dad!"

"Yelling's pointless," Freda said. "Your folks brought you here, and here you're going to stay." She kicked open a heavy metal door in front of them. "In you go. Make friends with that pathetic lot in there."

She thrust Scarlet and Cedric through the door, then shut and locked it with a squealy-sounding key.

They were in a dingy room whose metal walls were studded with rusty bolts. Neatly made hammocks were slung around the edges. In the middle was a group of twenty or more pirate children staring at them. Some were in the middle of playing cards, or marbles, or clapping games. Others were sitting at little desks made out of packing crates, writing out their homework in neat lines. Scarlet could tell at once that none of them was much good at pirating. Everyone was too quiet, and much too tidy-looking.

"I'm awfully sorry," said Horris, standing up from behind one of the packing-crate desks. "Are you all right? Freda can be quite rough sometimes."

"Freda scares me," said a gloomy girl pirate with a neat blue ribbon in her blonde hair.

"She's not called Freda the Fearless for nothing," said a very clean ginger-haired girl. "Nothing scares *her*. At least, nothing we know about. By the way, are those real sea-water stains on your pirate boots? And is that a real parrot dropping on your shoulder?"

"Parrots scare me," said the gloomy blue-ribboned girl pirate.

"Yes, my boots have real sea-water stains and I do have parrot poo on my shoulder," said Scarlet. "Well, budgie poo if you want to be picky about it."

Bluebeard flew off Scarlet's hat and landed on a steel girder near the ceiling. Several hundred mice already on the girder scurried out of his way.

"My brother and I are real pirates, you see," Scarlet continued.

"So why have you come to Gullible Grammar?" Horris asked. "It sounds like you don't need to learn much about pirating."

"We don't," Scarlet said patiently. "It's all a big mistake."

"I'm Molly," said the clean ginger-haired pirate. "It looks like you've already met Horris. And Catherine's the one with the blue ribbons. We call her Scaredy Cat because everything scares her."

Scarlet ran her fingers around the edge of the large metal door.

"It's locked," said Horris.

"So?" said Scarlet. "Cedric? Have you got that lock-picking gadget you mentioned earlier?"

Cedric pulled a long thin piece of metal out of his pocket and gave it to Scarlet. Scarlet stuck the lock-picker into the keyhole and jiggled it.

The pirate children all looked horrified.

"You can't do that," Horris said. "It's against the rules."

"That's your problem, Horris," Scarlet said kindly, jiggling the lock-picker again. "Proper pirates break rules."

Horris looked amazed. "You break rules?" he repeated.

"First basic fact of piracy," said Cedric. "Hasn't Freda the Fearless taught you that yet?"

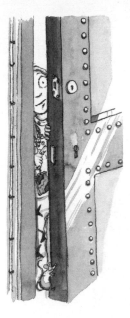

"She doesn't teach us much," Horris said. "She just shouts at us."

"Shouting scares me," said Scaredy Cat.

PLINK. Something gave way inside the door. Scarlet gave it a cautious push and peered outside.

Her heart sank as she saw Freda standing there with her arms folded across her massive chest.

"Breaking out already?" Freda boomed. "Looks like there's pirate blood in you after all, missy!"

"For the millionth time, we aren't supposed to be here," Scarlet shouted.

"You tell her, Scarlet!" Cedric said.

But as usual, Freda wasn't listening.

51

"Come along then," she bellowed. "Deck-swabbing practice!"

Miaow!

"THAT AIN'T SWABBING, HORRIS,"
Freda roared, pacing the oil-rig platform
as Scarlet, Cedric and the others swabbed
as hard as they could. "THAT'S
POLISHING! USE THE BRISTLY SIDE OF
YOUR SWABBING BRUSH, MOLLY!
YOU'RE THE MOST USELESS BUNCH OF
PIRATE KIDS I'VE EVER HAD TO
TEACH AT GULLIBLE GRAMMAR, AND
I'VE TAUGHT A FEW!"

Scaredy Cat kept bursting into tears, and Molly kept stopping every five swabs to brush the mouse poo off her knees. Horris said "Sorry" a lot and kept his head down.

"Everyone here is useless," Scarlet whispered to Cedric.

"With a teacher like that, I'm not

surprised," Cedric said. "I wish I'd brought my swabbing attachments, Scarlet. I could have put them on my splints and we'd have swabbed the whole place by now."

Scarlet sat back on her heels. The mice swarmed around her knees, and she batted them away. "Why are there so

many mice in this place?" she said.

"What Freda the Fearless needs is a cat," said Cedric.

"Freda won't allow it," Molly explained. "She really loves mice, see."

"She won't listen, she can't teach, and now she won't have a cat," Scarlet grumbled. "What next?"

Bluebeard flew down and settled on Scarlet's shoulder.

"You know what we need to do?" Scarlet said, feeling happier as she stroked Bluebeard's feathers. "We need to get rid of Freda the Fearless. And fast!"

Back on board *55 Ocean Drive*, the remainder of Scarlet's crew was having an emergency meeting. Ralph watched through half-closed eyes from his sunny spot by the ship's wheel.

"It's quite simple," said Lila. "We just march back up there and order that … *creature* to give our children back."

"I'll ask her to dance," said One-Eyed Scott with a hiccup. "She seemed like a charming lady."

"I'm getting really worried about One-Eyed Scott," said Grandpa Jack, wringing his hands.

"How are we going to get through those spiky teeth things?" Melvin said as he paced and down the deck.

"Knitting," said Grandpa Jack suddenly.

"Dad," said Lila. "We all know you love knitting, but I'm not sure that awful Freda woman will want one of your fish jumpers."

Grandpa Jack hurried down to his cabin. When he returned, he was holding three enormous bags full of wool. "We can wind my wool around those teeth things and make a net to climb over!" he said.

"That is an excellent idea," said Lila in astonishment.

"Up on high," Lipstick croaked from his position on Lila's shoulder.

"So what are we waiting for?" Melvin cried. "Let's go!"

"Miaow," said Ralph hopefully.

"OK, Ralph," said Melvin, scooping up the cat and tucking him under his arm. "You can come too. There's plenty of mice for you to chase on the oil rig."

Scarlet's knees ached from swabbing what felt like a hundred square miles of the oil-rig floor. But her ears ached even more. She'd never known anyone who could shout as loud, or for as long, as Freda the Fearless. Bluebeard had tucked his head under his wing after ten minutes of it. Scarlet wished she had a wing too, so she could do the same thing.

In addition to the deck-swabbing, they'd done knot-tying ("IF THAT'S A

KNOT, LEANNE, THEN I'M MY GREAT-AUNT MAUREEN!"), map-reading ("PIRATES SAY *PORT*, MOLLY, NOT *LEFT A BIT!*") and anchor-heaving ("WHAT DO YOU MEAN, ANCHORS SCARE YOU, CATHERINE?"). And Scarlet was quite sure that none of the pirate children had learned a single thing.

Freda had only said one thing worth listening to all day.

"LONG JOAN SILVER HERSELF INSPECTED THIS SCHOOL BEFORE SHE WAS SO TRAGICALLY EATEN BY THAT SHRIMP! SHE'D BE DISGUSTED AT THE SIGHT OF YOU!"

"Granny came to this oil rig!" Scarlet whispered in excitement to Cedric. "You know what that means, don't you? The third puzzle piece might be here!"

"But doesn't Gilbert Gauntlet have to be involved?" Cedric whispered back.

"He owns this place," Scarlet answered. "Didn't you see the logo on Freda's cutlass? That puzzle piece is here, or I'm a boiled banana."

"Right, you useless lot," Freda bellowed. "Time to practise our crow's-nest climbing."

Predictably, Scaredy Cat burst into

tears. "Heights scare me," she sobbed into Horris's shoulder.

Freda jabbed her thumb upwards. "See that crane?" she shouted. "I want you all up and down that like greased monkeys. Got it?"

Scarlet's eyes travelled up the enormous crane over their heads. It swayed gently, its chains going *clinkety-clunk* in the wind. Even the mice hadn't climbed it.

Nobody moved.

"GET A MOVE ON!" Freda roared. "WE AIN'T GOT ALL DAY!"

"It's awfully high," Horris said unhappily.

"THAT'S THE POINT!" Freda screamed.

Scarlet had a bright idea. If they could get Freda up the crane, perhaps they could trap her there.

"Why don't you show us how to do it, Freda?" she shouted, in her loudest voice.

Incredibly, Freda the Fearless heard her.

"I KNOW HOW TO DO IT, MISSY!" Freda shrieked. "IT'S YOU LOT WHO NEED TO PRACTISE!"

Something made Scarlet glance down the stretch of oil rig behind Freda. Lila, Melvin, Grandpa Jack and One-Eyed Scott were approaching, leaving a trail of brightly coloured wool behind them. Ralph was a happy blur at their feet, chasing a thousand mice in different directions.

Everyone stopped staring at the crane, and stared at the Silvers and One-Eyed Scott instead.

"What are you looking at?" Freda snapped.

63

She turned white as Ralph raced into view. The mice swarming around her ankles scattered like lightning, or shot up her trouser leg. Freda the Fearless gave her loudest shout ever.

"AIEEEEEE!"

And she hefted herself up on to the crane as fast as her enormous legs could carry her.

"OH," Freda moaned, scrambling upwards as Ralph stretched up to sniff at the mice in her trousers. "OH!"

Scarlet frowned. Freda didn't look as if she was protecting her beloved mice. More like she was protecting *herself*.

"I don't believe it," Cedric gasped. "Freda the Fearless is scared of *cats*!"

"Not so fearless after all, then," Scarlet grinned with delight.

Family Matters

Freda climbed the crane so fast that soon all they could see of her was her cutlass winking in the sunshine. Ralph meanwhile was so full of mice that he could hardly move. He settled down at the foot of the crane, where a shaft of sunshine had warmed up the metal platform nicely.

The pirate pupils of Gullible Grammar cheered in quiet voices. Then, realising

that no one was going to tell them off,
they cheered to the sky.

"Great timing, Mum!" Scarlet beamed,
running to hug her family.

"Why are you covered in wool?" asked
Cedric, looking puzzled.

"Don't worry about that!" Lila said,
pulling bits of pink wool out of her hair.
"The main thing is that we've rescued
you. And we've really got to go now,
Scarlet. We have to find a doctor for One-
Eyed Scott."

"Mice to see you," One-Eyed Scott

crooned, dancing around as dozens of little mice dashed between his feet. "To see you, mice … "

The pirate children had stopped cheering and were now clustered around Scarlet.

"Are you leaving?" asked Molly sadly.

"You can leave too if you like," Scarlet offered. "Freda will stay up that crane for as long as Ralph is there to guard it. We'll give you a lift on our ship."

"We'll take you anywhere you want to go," Cedric added.

"But we were just starting to learn some real pirate things from you," said Horris. "Like, how to break rules. Can't you stay for a bit longer? I've always wanted to know how to tie a proper pirate knot, and lead a proper pirate attack, and – well, everything really."

The other pirate children nodded eagerly.

"La la la," One-Eyed Scott warbled.

Scarlet hesitated. One-Eyed Scott still needed a doctor. But the useless young pirates of Gullible Grammar needed *her*!

"What do you want to do, Scarlet?" asked Grandpa Jack.

Scarlet took off her hat and rolled up her sleeves. "I think we can spare a few hours, Grandpa," she said. "Pass me that long piece of wool in your hair, will you? We're going to teach Horris and his friends how to tie a splice knot. We'll make pirates of you yet, Horris!"

Scarlet was amazed at how quickly
Horris and the others learned all her
pirate tricks. Lila demonstrated the best
knots, and Cedric the best grip to have
on a swabbing brush. Melvin performed
the hornpipe, and Grandpa Jack taught
the children some of One-Eyed Scott's
rudest pirate curses, which made several
mice leap off the oil rig and into the sea.

One-Eyed Scott meanwhile fell asleep at
the foot of Freda's crane with his head
resting on Ralph.

Molly stopped fretting about getting
dirt on her clothes. Scaredy Cat proved to
be brilliant at fearsome roaring. But
Horris was the best pupil of all. He
couldn't ask enough questions. What was
the best way to haul in an anchor? How

many pirate fibs could you tell before someone caught you out? Which end of a pirate ship was which?

"Enough!" Scarlet laughed, holding up her hands at Horris's questions. "Most of this stuff you have to learn when you're out at sea, Horris."

"Can we sail on your ship, Scarlet?" Horris asked eagerly.

"Yay!" shouted the others.

"Of course you can," said Scarlet. "There's just one more thing I have to teach you. Real crow's-nest climbing."

There was another crane on the far side of the rig which looked ideal for crow's-nest climbing. Scarlet put her foot at the bottom and began to climb.

"Hand over hand!" Scarlet shouted down to the children below. "Foot over foot! Don't look down and you can't go wrong, I promise!"

Halfway up, she grabbed on to a wire and slid back down to the oil platform with a grin.

"Oooh!" shouted the pupils of Gullible Grammar.

"There's nothing to it," Scarlet said as Bluebeard fluttered proudly around her hat in a whirl of blue and yellow.

"Me next!" Horris cried. He jumped on to the crane.

"You don't have to climb all the way to the top if you don't want to!" Scarlet called, shading her eyes to watch Horris's progress.

"It's fantastic up here!" Horris shouted, scrambling nimbly up the crane's long metal neck. "I can see the whole of the sea!"

He arrived at the top to tremendous applause from Scarlet and the others down below.

"And I shall now slide down again!" Horris announced. He was about to take hold of the long wire when he stopped. "Hey," he said, peering at something on the very top of the crane. "What's this?"

He held up a tiny something that sparkled blue in the sunshine.

Scarlet's heart lurched. She clutched at the square green pendant around her throat, dizzy with excitement. *Up on high...*

Horris grabbed the wire and slid down to the ground, clutching the sparkly blue thing in his hand. He showed it to Scarlet. It was a piece of blue enamel, with two straight edges and one wavy edge.

Somehow, Long Joan Silver had put the third puzzle piece of the tremendous treasure hunt on the top of the oil-rig's crane!

"The third puzzle piece!" Cedric shouted triumphantly.

"Yahoo!" Grandpa Jack yelled, while Melvin and Lila danced up and down around One-Eyed Scott.

"Up on high," Lipstick squawked approvingly.

"I don't know what puzzle Cedric's talking about," said Horris, "but you can have it if you like, Scarlet."

Scarlet took the sparkly puzzle piece. "You don't know what this means to us, Horris," she said. "How can we thank you?"

"You don't have to thank *me*," Horris said. "I should be thanking *you*! Right now, I feel like I could ambush a whole pirate ship by myself." He paused. "In fact," he said, "why don't we do that, right now?"

Scarlet clipped the puzzle piece carefully on to her pendant and stared at the young pirate. "You want to do an ambush?" she said. "That's pretty advanced piracy, Horris."

"I reckon I could do it," said Horris. He

turned to the other pirate children. "Who'll help me?"

"We will!" the others shouted.

"GARR!" said Scaredy Cat, making Ralph jump and wake up One-Eyed Scott.

"Who are we going to ambush?" said Molly breathlessly.

"I know the perfect pirate," said Horris. "The owner of Gullible Grammar, Gilbert Gauntlet himself, is coming to inspect the school tonight. We could ambush *him*."

"*Gilbert Gauntlet!*" Scarlet and her crew all gasped together.

"A lovely gentleman," said One-Eyed Scott. "La la la."

"How do you know Gilbert Gauntlet is coming today, Horris?" Scarlet asked.

"Because he's my dad," said Horris.

Ambush!

"Gilbert Gauntlet is your *father*?" said Lila in horror.

"Now you mention it, I can see the likeness," said Cedric.

It was true. Horris had the same blond hair as his father, and the same blue eyes. He was just a bit smaller.

"I'm not proud of it," Horris said. "It's just a fact. I was an embarrassment to him, so he set up Gullible Grammar to

get me out of the way. Freda
worked for him as a brickie
when he was in the building
trade. I've been here since I
was six years old."

Up near the top of the crane,
Freda was still whimpering.

Ralph yawned and sharpened his claws on the crane's base.

"I've got a brilliant plan," said Horris. "It's something I've wanted to do for ages. I'll need your ship, though." He took a deep breath. "Will you trust me, Scarlet?" he asked.

Scarlet felt uneasy. Horris was lovely – but he *was* her arch-enemy's son. She bit her lip and glanced at her crew. "What do you think?" she said.

"Tum tee tum," said One-Eyed Scott.

"I think Horris is all right," said Grandpa Jack.

"He might look like his dad, but otherwise he's totally different," Cedric said in agreement.

"How can you be sure?" Lila demanded.

Melvin took Lila's hand. He looked unconvinced as well.

Scarlet counted. Two crew members were for Horris. Two were against. One-Eyed Scott was still too bonkers to count. So the decision lay with her.

"Horris?" Scarlet said at last. "*55 Ocean Drive* is all yours."

Scarlet made sure that everyone was on board before she called Ralph away from the crane. Freda started climbing down as fast as she could, but *55 Ocean Drive* had cast off before she was halfway to the ground.

"See how you like shouting at nobody, Freda!" Scarlet yelled gleefully as *55 Ocean Drive* sailed away from the oil rig.

With twenty new crew members all

keen to experience life on a real pirate ship, *55 Ocean Drive* got a complete makeover. The decks were scrubbed till they squeaked. The spokes on the ship's wheel were waxed and polished. Dazzling Doris the ship's figurehead was freshly painted, and the sails were washed and ironed to perfection.

But not everyone was happy. Lila played gloomy pirate music on her accordion as the sun went down, and Melvin busied himself in the galley so that he didn't have to talk to Horris. Cedric and Grandpa Jack, however, netted more than thirty fish between them to feed their new crew members. Scarlet oversaw everything, her heart see-sawing in all directions. What if she was wrong about Horris after all?

"If Gilbert Gauntlet is planning on reaching the oil rig tonight, then we should see him soon," said Scarlet at last, tossing her supper fishbones over the side of the ship.

"Even though it's getting dark?" Molly asked.

"Dad always lights up his ship like a fairground ride," said Horris. "So everyone knows he's coming. He can be a real idiot."

As Horris spoke, a row of blazing ship's lights appeared on the horizon.

"I'm sorry about this, Scarlet," said Horris, "but I've got to lock you and your family in the brig now."

"How do we know you'll let us out again?" Lila demanded.

"I can't *make* you trust me," said

Horris. "All I can do is *ask* you."

There was a tense silence.

"Pieces of eight!" Bluebeard squawked, flying off Scarlet's hat and landing on Horris's shoulder.

"If Bluebeard trusts him, then so should we," Scarlet told her crew firmly. "Into the brig!"

The brig was near the prow of the ship. Horris fixed a bright lantern overhead so that the Silvers, One-Eyed Scott, Ralph, Lipstick and Bluebeard could all be clearly seen in the darkness. The door clicked into place, and Horris turned the key with an awful clunk.

Scarlet's heart was in her mouth as Horris looked at her from outside the brig. Had this been the worst mistake of her pirate career?

Horris grinned and passed the key through the bars. "Told you that you could trust me," he said as Scarlet seized the key and the Silvers whooped with relief. "You'll know when to let yourself out. All you Gullible Grammar lot, listen to me!"

The other young pirates gathered around Horris.

"Can everyone swim?" Horris asked. "How about you, Scaredy Cat?"

"Swimming doesn't scare me," said Scaredy Cat firmly.

"I need you all to climb over the side and tread water for a bit. Wait for my signal – two splashes of the oar – to start swimming towards my dad's ship," said Horris.

"Aye, aye Horris!" shouted the Gullible Grammar pupils, before throwing themselves eagerly overboard.

"He's good," said Melvin, stroking Ralph and beaming.

"He had a good teacher," Lila said fondly, patting Scarlet on the leg.

The lights from Gilbert Gauntlet's luxury yacht, *The Glove*, were dazzling now. Scarlet couldn't help shivering as she saw the billowing purple sails and shining white prow.

"Here goes," said Horris, heaving the ship's dinghy over the side and jumping aboard. "Dad!" he shouted, rowing across the strip of sea that separated *55 Ocean Drive* from *The Glove*. "Hey, Dad! It's me, Horris!"

Gilbert Gauntlet emerged from his luxurious cabin. His blond hair gleamed like gold in the lamplight, and his buttons shone like diamonds. "Horris?" he said, looking astonished. "Why aren't you at school, boy?"

"I've escaped, Dad!" Horris called, rowing steadily towards *The Glove*. "And guess what? I've got my own pirate ship now! These pirates called the Silvers sailed up to school in their ship, and I ambushed them! You can see the ship behind me. Aren't you proud?"

"My dear boy!" Gilbert Gauntlet gasped. "You really captured the *Silvers*?"

"See for yourself," said Horris, waving behind him at the brightly lit brig.

"Start groaning, everyone," Scarlet hissed.

"Oh, oh, oh," Lila and Cedric moaned dramatically.

"Woe, oh woe," howled Melvin and Grandpa Jack.

"Three men went to mow," sang One-Eyed Scott.

Gilbert Gauntlet roared with delight. "I have to see this properly, dear boy! Are you taking visitors?"

"Hop aboard, Dad," Horris coaxed. "Bring your crew if you like."

"Dennis!" Gilbert Gauntlet shouted. "Desmond! Derek! Duncan! … My son here has just pulled off the finest ambush in the history of the Seven Seas! My own son! He has that ghastly girly's ship!"

It said a great deal for Scarlet's reputation that the whole of Gilbert Gauntlet's crew rushed off *The Glove* and into Horris's dinghy to see the captives for themselves.

"Yes!" Gilbert Gauntlet cried as Horris rowed steadily back towards *55 Ocean Drive*. "I can see them! The girly's there, it's true! You silly little Silvers. You've lost me a lot of business. Now it's payback time!"

Horris splashed the water twice with his oar. Gilbert Gauntlet was too busy laughing to notice as twenty little pirate heads started swimming towards *The Glove*.

"Crow all you want, Gauntlet!" shouted Grandpa Jack, trying hard not to grin.

"We'll get you back for this!"

"And just how do you think you'll do that from inside your cage?" Gilbert Gauntlet purred.

Scarlet could see twenty wet young pirates swarming up the ropes of *The Glove*. Molly's thumbs-up was silhouetted against the moon.

"*He's* not going to get you back," said Horris,

jumping up. "But *I* am."

Gilbert Gauntlet frowned as Horris leaped overboard and swam back to *The Glove*. Molly and Scaredy Cat helped him out of the water.

"HORRIS!" Gilbert Gauntlet bellowed. "Get back here and explain!"

"NOW!" shouted Scarlet, unlocking the brig.

The Silvers burst on to the deck of *55 Ocean Drive*.

"Lock me up and throw away the key," One-Eyed Scott warbled. "OUCH!"

The brig's heavy door had whacked him very hard on the forehead.

"Oh please, not another bang on the brain!" Lila groaned. "I can't take any more cheerfulness!"

One-Eyed Scott staggered to his feet.

His chicken bones clattered around his ears. "What the blasting blazes is that purple pimple Gauntlet doing in our dinghy?" he demanded.

"Scott, you old bloater-breath!" Grandpa Jack roared joyfully. "You're back!"

Scarlet waved the ship's keys at Gilbert Gauntlet and his open-mouthed crew, and jigged a victory dance. "You're the one who just got ambushed, Gauntlet," she sang. "Not us!"

"Whee!" Cedric chortled.

"WHAAAAAT!" Gilbert Gauntlet shrieked.

The little dinghy wobbled from side to side, and the worst pirate on the Seven Seas was forced to sit down rather suddenly. Scarlet had never seen him so angry.

"You're in deep water, Gauntlet," Melvin chuckled. "Literally!"

"I re-name this ship *The Gullible*!" Horris shouted, swinging from the prow of his dad's luxury yacht. "Thanks for sending me to Gullible Grammar, Dad. I'd never have become a pirate if it hadn't been for you and Scarlet Silver!"

"HORRIS GAUNTLET!" Gilbert Gauntlet shrieked. "COME BACK HERE! I DISOWN YOU! YOU … "

Words failed the pirate as he watched

his own son cheerfully turn the wheel of the newly named *The Gullible* and sail off in the opposite direction. Scarlet almost felt sorry for him. But not sorry enough to rescue him.

As *55 Ocean Drive* sailed away, leaving Gilbert Gauntlet shouting at his henchmen to start rowing somewhere – "ANYWHERE!" – Lila started playing the jolly tune of *Up on High*. Scarlet clutched the pendant and its three pieces around her neck. Just one more piece to go – and Long Joan Silver's tremendous treasure would be theirs!

"*Up on high, up on high,*
Sunshine smoothies, seagull pie,
Tap your toes, 'cos we know why
Granny Joan said up on high!"

HB 978 0 340 98912 8
PB 978 0 340 95967 1

HB 978 0 340 98913 5
PB 978 0 340 95968 8

HB 978 0 340 98914 2
PB 978 0 340 95969 5

HB 978 0 340 98916 6
PB 978 0 340 95971 8

HB 978 0 340 98917 3
PB 978 0 340 95972 5

Read more of Scarlet Silver's adventures on the High Seas